MAGNUS
the Naughty Dog
Steals Lunch

Written by
Carrie Torgersen

Illustrated by
Eleonore Sebastian

BEAVER'S POND PRESS
SAINT PAUL

To Victoria,
for loving my children,
for tolerating my crazy,
for being strong where I am weak,
I am forever grateful.

—Carrie

For Mocha,
a forever puppy who is
forever in our hearts.

—Eleonore

Magnus the Naughty Dog Steals Lunch © 2021 by Carrie Torgersen

Cover and interior illustrations by Eleonore Sebastian
Book design and typesetting by Dan Pitts
Managing Editor: Laurie Buss Herrmann

ISBN 13: 978-1-64343-945-7
Library of Congress Catalog Number: 2019942309
Printed in the United States of America
First Printing: 2020
24 23 22 21 20   5 4 3 2 1

Beaver's Pond Press
939 West Seventh Street
Saint Paul, MN 55102
(952) 829-8818
www.BeaversPondPress.com

To order, visit carrietorgersenbooks.com. Reseller discounts available.

Contact Carrie Torgersen at carrietorgersenbooks.com for school visits, speaking engagements, book club discussions, and interviews.

Our family lives in a house in the woods.

Almost every day, Mom and Dad go to work.

Almost every day, our nanny takes care of us and Magnus.

Magnus is a Vizsla dog.

That means he has ALL KINDS of ENERGY . . . ALL the time.

He is a beautiful brown color and he has big floppy ears.

Magnus does not like to listen. Magnus likes to chase cats.

And to get up on the kitchen counters.

He also loves . . .

FOOD!

Except for vegetables . . . and avocados.

One beautiful summer day, we made the perfect picnic lunch.

And set it on the car.

Magnus tried and tried,
but he could not leave the basket alone.
He climbed up on the car to get a closer look.

And the food smelled so wonderful,
he could not help himself.

He ate the whole lunch! Plastic and all!

At first we were very angry!

And then we were very sad.

Magnus ran away as FAST as he could,

which was REALLY SUPER FAST!

Eventually he had to stop running . . .

and start feeling.

When he stood still,
he felt bad.
Actually,
he felt terrible.

And he realized
that he was sorry for what he had done.

So he came back to apologize.

At first we were not ready to forgive him.

But then our nanny reminded us
that when we don't forgive,
it hurts us too,
and we feel bad inside.

So we all forgave Magnus, and we all felt better inside.

At least until the next time.